A rushing noise filled my ears as my heart began to pound. I tore the pin from the grenade and pulled back my arm to hurl it. I heard a CRACK! and felt a blow just above the elbow. The grenade was torn from my hand and hurtled away, heading back down the slope. I struggled to retain my balance in the shifting sand, desperately trying to pull another grenade out. Then I felt an explosion in my chest and I slumped to my knees in agony.

Read and collect the other books in the
Warpath *series*

WARPATH 8
Island of Fear

J. ELDRIDGE

A fictional story
based on real-life events

PUFFIN BOOKS

PUFFIN BOOKS

Published by the Penguin Group
Penguin Books Ltd, 80 Strand, London WC2R 0RL, England
Penguin Putnam Inc., 375 Hudson Street, New York, New York 10014, USA
Penguin Books Australia Ltd, 250 Camberwell Road, Camberwell, Victoria 3124, Australia
Penguin Books Canada Ltd, 10 Alcorn Avenue, Toronto, Ontario, Canada M4V 3B2
Penguin Books India (P) Ltd, 11 Community Centre, Panchsheel Park, New Delhi – 110 017, India
Penguin Books (NZ) Ltd, Cnr Rosedale and Airborne Roads, Albany, Auckland, New Zealand
Penguin Books (South Africa) (Pty) Ltd, 24 Sturdee Avenue, Rosebank 2196, South Africa

Penguin Books Ltd, Registered Offices: 80 Strand, London WC2R 0RL, England

www.penguin.com

First published 2000
5

Text copyright © Jim Eldridge, 2000
Photographs copyright © the Imperial War Museum
All rights reserved

The moral right of the author has been asserted

Set in Bookman Old Style

Printed in England by Clays Ltd, St Ives plc

British Library Cataloguing in Publication Data
A CIP catalogue record for this book is available from the British Library

ISBN 0-141-30733-1

Contents

The War in the Pacific

By December 1941 the Second World War had been going on for over two years, with Germany dominating a mostly occupied Europe, supported by its ally, Italy. During that time the USA had remained neutral. Then, on 7 December 1941, without prior warning, Japanese bombers attacked the American fleet at Pearl Harbor on the Pacific island of Hawaii. (Japan was an ally of Germany.) It was an act that brought the USA into the war.

Although America committed many of its forces to the war in Europe and North Africa, it was the Japanese who were seen as the main threat. As a result, a large part of the American war effort was in the Pacific.

By mid-1944, following the successful D-Day landings in France, Italy had surrendered and Germany was on the defensive. Japanese forces had dug in on many of the Pacific islands, forming a solid ring of defence around their homeland.

The US had tried bombarding the Japanese defences, both from battleships and from planes, but they had proved impregnable to such attacks. If the Japanese were to be overcome there was only one way to do it – by putting marines ashore to take each island one by one. It was a deadly strategy.

The key island was Iwo Jima. Before any attack on it could even be considered, the surrounding Marianas Islands had to be taken – Saipan, Tinian and Guam.

Our story begins in June 1944 as one young marine experiences combat for the first time against the Japanese forces on the island of Saipan.

US Marines Kit List

(Marine Corps field-pack combination)

- Haversack/ knapsack
- Long blanket roll
- Shelter half
  (a section of canvas for shelter,
  like half a tent)
- Gas mask
- Two filled canteens of water
- A unit of fire
- Fragmentation grenades
- Smoke grenades
- Two rounds of 60 mm mortar
  ammunition
- Personal weapons
  e.g.
  a service .45 pistol

  Thompson sub-machine-gun

  2 x 35-round magazine cartridges
  taped to the end of the weapon

  4 x 35-round magazine cartridges
  on pistol belt

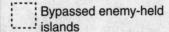

Map of the Pacific Islands
Strategic Situation
February 1945

- ⌐ ⌐ Bypassed enemy-held
  ⌐⌐⌐ islands

- ⟹ Allied Advance

- ■ Japanese-controlled Islands

- ⦂⦂⦂ Mainland

- ▨ Allied-controlled Islands

Wake Island

Eniwetok

Kwajalein

PACIFIC
OCEAN

MARSHALL ISLANDS

New Ireland

Bougainville

SOLOMON ISLANDS

Sea-to-shore Vehicles Used by the Marines for Beach Landings

LVTs – Landing vehicles with caterpillar tracks, enabling them to come out of the water and continue across soft sand. Used for getting troops on to land. Also known as amphtracs (amphibious vehicles tracked).

LVT(A)s – Armoured amphibious tractors with a crew of four. Looked like a tank, but capable of being both an armoured boat and a tank on land. Armament:
1 x 75 mm gun; 1 x M-3 howitzer; 2 x .50-in Browning machine-guns.

LSTs – Landing ships carrying tanks.

LSMs – Landing ships, medium. Carried tanks and bulldozers.

LCVPs – Ramped boats which carried anti-tank guns, half-track vehicles, Jeeps, etc.

The battle for Iwo Jima was one of the bloodiest fought by the US Marines. Many men died. I survived ... just. This is my story.

John Smith
US Marines

Chapter 1
Attack on Saipan

The noise of the battle was deafening. Gun and mortar fire from the Japanese defences poured down on us. Around me, marines crumpled on the soft sand of the beach as the enemy fire took its toll. The bombardment from our own ships lying offshore continued, the thud of our bombs and rockets shaking the ground beneath me, as if earthquake after earthquake were hitting the island.

I'm John Smith of the US Marines, 18 years old, and this was my first real experience of combat. Months of training at boot camp and lectures from our instructors had done their best to prepare us, but I now realized that nothing could prepare you for the real thing. This was win or die. This was a living nightmare.

We'd hit the beach of Saipan at 0855. As

we'd run from our LVT and dived for what little cover the beach had to offer, the Japanese had opened up from their defensive positions. Now we were pinned down. As bullets smacked into the sand around me, I struggled hard to control the sense of fear that threatened to overcome me. I kept muttering to myself, 'You can survive this! You can survive this!'

Not being able to advance, we began to dig in, making holes in the sand as cover. Digging-in is hard enough to do at the best of times, but almost impossible when you're lying face-down, aware that if you put your head up too high a bullet could hit you. I was lucky: I'd managed to get behind a ridge of raised sand that gave me some cover, not much though.

I looked over at Paddy Riley, who was also lying as flat as he could behind a ridge of sand. He gave me a big wink as if to say, 'Don't worry, buddy, we can get out of this.' I couldn't believe he looked so calm. But then, that was Paddy's way. Paddy was big in every sense: the way he looked, the way he thought, the way he acted. He was over six feet tall, broad-shouldered, very fit and also very fast for someone of his size. He seemed to be able to brush aside any obstacle he came across. With his jet-black hair cropped short, marine style, his broken nose slightly askew (a reminder of his days as a boxer back in civilian life) and his cheerful grin, Paddy was a tonic. When things looked bad, Paddy could always be counted on to cheer you up. As the battle raged around me though, even Paddy's confidence couldn't reassure me.

This first wave of our assault on Saipan had begun at 0700 hours on 15 June 1944. Although, in reality, the actual attack had started some time before. For the last four days our aircraft-carriers and battleships had kept up a steady bombardment of the island, pounding it with shells and rockets, trying to knock out the enemy defences. They'd done their best, but the Japanese had had years to build really solid pillboxes and gun emplacements.

At 0730, we'd begun disembarking into our LVTs. The aim had been for our LVTs to come out of the sea, on to the beach and right up to the Japanese positions, under covering fire of our aircraft and battleships. As we came in to shore, it

11

became apparent that this wasn't going to be easy. The Japanese shells were hitting dangerously close. I saw two LVTs go down near us, marines tumbling out into the water and sinking beneath the waves, loaded down by the weight of their packs.

The shells that missed exploded in the sea around us, creating huge great geysers that swamped our landing-craft. As we neared the beach, we hit the coral reef. The LVT I was in managed to find a passage through it to the beach. Others weren't so lucky and got stuck on the reef, becoming sitting targets for Japanese fire. As the vehicle I was in came out of the water on to the beach, it took a direct hit that tore off its caterpillar tracks and we ground to a shuddering halt.

'Hit the beach!' Sergeant Sykes had shouted.

Despite shaking with fear, I had managed to run with the others, ducking and dodging, bullets flying all around us. Lying behind a ridge of sand desperately trying to stay calm, I couldn't believe I had even made it to the beach. Eight thousand marines had set out in this first wave. Thinking of the casualties lying on the beach and out there on the reef, I wondered just how many of us had made it this far.

'Smith! Riley!'

I turned my head and saw Sergeant Sykes crawling as fast as he could through the soft sand towards Paddy and me.

'Sir?' I responded.

Sykes was a guy I had a lot of time for. Put some men in command and they seem to forget what it's like to be an ordinary soldier. Not Sykes. As tough as they come, but fair. Short in stature, his cropped hair was already grey, even though he was only in his early thirties.

Sykes reached us and gestured with his thumb at a point up ahead of us.

'There's a sniper up there, holed up in a pillbox,' he said. 'He's got himself well dug in. I need two men to go and take him out.'

'Sounds like we're the two men, sarge,' grinned Paddy.

I felt a sick feeling deep in my stomach as Paddy said the words. I knew that Paddy didn't feel fear the same way as I did, but the real problem was that he thought other people were just like him. For Paddy, being in battle was excitement and adventure. For me, it was fear of being killed or badly wounded.

'That's what I thought,' nodded Sykes. 'I'm going to open a barrage of fire from over there, behind the ridge.' He indicated a point about a hundred yards away. 'With a bit of luck that might blind-side him and keep him occupied enough to give you time to get up there. At least near enough to get some grenades in. The fact is, fellas, if we don't take that guy out, we're stuck on this beach and ain't going nowhere.'

'Leave it to us, sarge,' I said.

Although my words sounded brave, I hoped any quaver in my voice didn't give me away. The ridge of sand between me and the enemy was my only protection and in a few seconds I would have to leave it and make for that pillbox. 'This is what you've trained for,' I whispered to myself in encouragement.

'Go when we start our diversionary fire,' Sergeant Sykes said.

'Yes, sir,' Paddy and I nodded.

With that, Sykes turned and crawled back to join the other members of the platoon.

'Looks like we get to be heroes,' smiled Paddy.

I swallowed hard, doing my best not to show him how scared I was. I liked Paddy a lot. Out of all the guys in the platoon, he was the one I'd describe as my best buddy. But at this moment I was cursing him and his constant desire to get into the hottest point of any battle. I forced a grin back at Paddy.

'Someone's got to be heroes, might as well be us,' I replied.

We lay there, rifles ready, our attention now on Sykes as he reached the others. The deafening noise of battle meant we had no way of hearing what he was saying to them, but their nods and the cocking of their guns told us that this was our moment. Sykes looked towards us and gave a thumbs up. I uttered a silent prayer as I signalled back to him. Sykes issued his instructions and the men began firing blindly over the ridge, up towards where the sniper was holed up.

'That's us!' said Paddy. 'Here goes nothing!' and he darted off.

Doing my best to hold back my fear, I followed him up the dune, keeping my

15

head low to avoid the sniper's bullets. Above us I could see the concrete pillbox set into the ground. A rifle poked through one of the slits and it was firing.

Paddy stumbled and fell to the ground. My instinct was to help, but I knew I had to leave him. I passed him, my teeth clenched tight shut with determination. I was nearing the pillbox now. I could see the vertical openings, with long grass hanging down to conceal them. Scrambling forward, I pulled a hand-grenade from my pack with my free hand.

Suddenly a rifle poked through the dark slit above me, and my blood froze. A rushing noise filled my ears as my heart began to pound. I tore the pin from the grenade and pulled back my arm to hurl it. I heard a CRACK! and felt a blow just above the elbow. The grenade was torn from my hand and hurtled away, heading back down the slope.

I struggled to keep my balance in the shifting sand while desperately trying to pull out another grenade from my pack. Then I felt an explosion in my chest and I slumped to my knees in agony. As my eyes lost focus, I felt myself crash to the ground.

Chapter 2
Hit

When I came to I was back on the beach. A corpsman was bending over me, tying a huge dressing to my chest with bandages. I opened my mouth, trying to ask him how I was, but no words came out. My mouth felt like it was stuffed with cotton wool. The corpsman realized that I was awake.

'Save your breath from talking, kid. You're gonna need all you've got for breathing,' he grunted.

An explosion rocked the ground beneath me and sent a shower of sand raining down on us. The corpsman ducked his head to keep the sand out of his eyes, then carried on bandaging me.

'As soon as we can we're gonna get you off this beach,' he told me. 'Right now you're safer here. We try and haul you out now, you're gonna die for sure.'

I was dimly aware of him tying off the bandage, then there was another huge explosion and everything around me was blotted out again.

The rest was just a haze. Every now and then I floated back into consciousness to make out a change in events. At one time I felt myself being carried and heard the splash of water around me. Then I was rocking backwards and forwards. All the time I was aware of a dull pain in my chest and my right arm that sometimes seemed to fill my whole body with agony.

When I finally came round it seemed as if the whole room was going up and down. Then my head cleared and I realized the room really was going up and down. I was on a ship. I tried to focus my eyes and get my bearings through the fog that filled my brain. I was on our hospital ship. I'd been on it before, but only for the occasional small wound, nothing serious. Now I was bandaged up like an Egyptian mummy. Drip tubes connected my body to bottles suspended by the side of my bed.

'He's awake!' came a voice near by.

I tried to turn my head to see who it was,

but a pain shot through my neck as I did so.

'Easy, John boy!' came a familiar voice.

Then Paddy Riley came into view, a broad grin on his face. His left arm was in plaster from shoulder to wrist.

'Paddy,' I managed to say. 'I saw you go down. I thought you were dead.'

Paddy shook his head with an apologetic grin.

'Not me,' he said ruefully. 'Just plain clumsy. I slipped on that volcanic ash they call sand. Man, that's treacherous stuff! A guy can't get a footing on stuff like that.'

I gestured at the plaster on his arm. He shrugged.

'I got this later. After I took out the pillbox.'

I struggled to remember. It was all so vague. The concrete pillbox. Me, running up towards it. The barrel of the rifle poking out straight at me.

'When you went down I thought you was a gonner for sure,' continued Paddy. 'Anyway, I upped and let 'em have two grenades right through those holes. That did it! But it was thanks to you, going for them in the first place.'

My head hurt and I could feel myself drifting. There was so much I wanted to ask Paddy. What had happened to the other members of our platoon? Had we won? Was the island ours? What about the other Marianas Islands? But everything was swimming out of focus and, despite my struggling against it, I lost consciousness again.

Chapter 3
Hospital Ship

It was a few more days before I was conscious enough to find out the whole story. Apparently my wooziness hadn't been caused by my injury, but by the drugs the medical corps had pumped into me to keep me under.

This time, when Paddy came visiting, I was able to act and talk more sensibly.

'You took a bullet in the chest,' Paddy told me. 'Lucky for you it was on the right-hand side. They had to patch your lung up. If it had been on the other side they'd have been trying to put your heart back together. So, you've got a few cracked ribs, smashed collarbone, and a big hole in your back where the bullet came out.'

'How do you know all this?'

'I bribed the corpsman to let me look at your file,' grinned Paddy. 'I told him I

21

needed to know if my buddy was gonna die so I could fix up a collection for the funeral before all the other guys got split up.'

I chuckled. It hurt all over, but at least I was alive. I felt an overwhelming sense of relief. I'd been in battle for the first time, I'd been wounded, but I'd survived. I was still alive!

'What happened after I got hit?'

'We did good,' said Paddy. 'The top brass are very impressed. Once again, the marines are winning the war for Uncle Sam.'

'Forget all that, just give me the details,' I said impatiently. 'Like, how long have I been here?'

'OK,' nodded Paddy. 'Five days, is the answer to that one.'

'And the enemy?'

'On the run. Not that there are many places to run on that island. Trust me, Saipan is as good as ours. Word is, we're gonna finish it, then take the rest of the Marianas – Tinian and Guam. Then it's full speed for Tokyo.' He patted the plaster on his arm. 'I just hope this is working by then. I'd sure hate to miss the big one.'

*

In fact it took a little longer for the conquest of the Marianas than Paddy anticipated. I lay in my sick bed ticking the days off the calendar and listening to reports coming back to the ship from the combat troops. As the days turned into weeks, I was able to follow the action by talking to the other soldiers and piecing together scraps of reports from the medical orderlies. It turned out that after that first assault, it took ten days, until 25 June, before the main peak on Saipan, Mount Tapotchu, was captured. It was nearly another two weeks, 7 July, before the island was finally won by our boys. In the campaign to take Saipan, the Japanese lost 26,000 men. Our casualties were 3,500 dead and 13,000 wounded. Including me.

As I lay in my bed in the floating hospital I saw more and more men come in, wounded or dying. I was getting stronger by the day, and I knew that sooner or later some MO was gonna kick me back to a bunk, because they needed the space for all the new casualties.

It was a time of mixed feelings. As I watched the wounded come in, a part of me wanted to be out there, helping them try to win this war. But another part of me just wanted to get out of this war alive, and I had to guiltily admit to myself that I was relieved to be safe on the hospital ship, out of combat.

Finally, by the end of July, word came through that Tinian had also been taken and the marines were now setting their sights on the third island, Guam. Reinforcement ships had arrived and our hospital ship was stood down and headed back home. All men with 'less serious' wounds were transferred to the ships that were staying, so that they could be patched up and returned to battle. These 'walking wounded' included Paddy, whose arm was almost healed, so we said goodbye and he returned to battle.

My wounds were considered serious, so I was among those who were to be sent back to the good old US of A to await a full recovery. I still had a hole in my chest, a hole in my back and a right lung that sounded like a leaky bellows if I breathed too hard. But I was alive. And I was going home.

Chapter 4

Stateside

Back at camp, it took several weeks of briefings and de-briefings and medical checks before the MOs decided it would be cheaper and less of a problem for the Marine Corps if I did my convalescing at my parents' home in Kalamazoo, Michigan.

Kalamazoo is a small kind of town. Basically, it's a long stretch of railway track with single-storey houses and buildings alongside. One way the track goes to Chicago, the other way leads to New York. Mostly, people pass straight through on their way to one of those two cities. Very few people actually get off the train in Kalamazoo.

Like most American towns, Kalamazoo is full of families who came from somewhere else. English, Irish, German,

Scots, Dutch. Mom and Pop live in a little clapboard house on the outskirts, out towards Comstock. Just around the corner live my father's parents, Otto and Gretel Smith. My father's name is Charles, although he'd been christened Karl. My grandparents had changed his first name when they'd changed their surname from Krupp to Smith. Yup, we Smiths are actually Germans.

Early in the twentieth century, my grandpappy Otto and his wife had come over to America to settle and start a new life. With them they brought their son, young Karl. My pop. The Krupp family. Then, in 1914 war broke out in Europe. Germany against everybody else. In 1916 the USA came into the war and Germany became America's most bitter enemy. Rather than let his family suffer because of their German name, Grandpappy Otto took drastic action and decided that his family were going to have a proper *American* name. So he chose Smith. Which, I'm told, is English. Still, it's a nice simple name with no troubled connections. And that's what Grandpappy Otto was looking for in 1916. We weren't the only ones. Lots of German families did this, even the British Royal family: up till the First World War their family name had been Saxe-Coburg-Gotha but it was then changed to Windsor.

To an outsider the situation may seem strange. Here we were, fighting a war in Europe against Germans and Italians. Yet our combat troops included men from Italian and German families. Personally, I consider myself an American and fighting for my country was the right thing to do.

I was the only person to get off the train at Kalamazoo. I caught a cab and as it pulled up outside my parents' house, they were already rushing out of the door to greet me.

'John!' squealed my mom.

I just had time to remind her that I was still convalescing before she smothered me in an enormous hug. Within minutes of my arrival home, word had spread and half the neighbourhood started calling. To listen to my mom talk as she handed round cakes and coffee, anyone would have thought I'd taken the whole Marianas Islands single-handed!

For the next few weeks I rested and

recovered in Kalamazoo. As each day passed, the horror of what I had seen in Saipan faded and with it my sense of fear. Everything returned to what it had been before I went off to join the marines. The only sour note for me was when Mom came home one day from the store with our groceries and chattily said: 'I ran into Mrs Pelt today. Henry's home on leave. He's in the marines now, just like you.'

I could imagine Mom proudly telling Mrs Pelt how brave her son John was, and how I'd been injured.

'Do you remember when you were both at school and he got you into trouble for fighting?' Mom continued. 'At least he's turned out well now.'

I didn't answer her. Mom is the kind of person who will always try to find something good to say about anyone. For me, Henry Pelt had always been a dumb jock who bullied other people. Despite what Mom said, I felt sure he was probably just the same now.

Henry and I were opposites. When we were at school he was a sports jock, built like a brick wall even when he was young, the star of all the sports teams. Me, I was kinda shortish and I preferred reading to sports. I was good at math and English and all that kind of stuff. I don't think Henry ever read a book. Not for pleasure, anyway. The fact that he wasn't too bright probably wouldn't have bothered Henry if it wasn't for the fact that his dad insisted he was the best at everything – including his studies. He gave Henry a really hard time about his poor grades and, as a result, Henry took it out on me the only way he knew how, physically.

Although I was small, I was fast. After one particular scrap between us in the school yard, when I'd actually given Henry a bloody nose, he decided it didn't look good, a big sports jock like him getting punched by a bookworm like me. So he tried a different way to have a go at me. When news started to come through from Europe about what was going on in Germany, Henry had his new weapon.

It was no secret that our family had once been called Krupp and came from Germany. My Grandmom Gretel still spoke English with a thick German accent. And so Henry started calling me 'The Nazi'. I'd been too young to really understand the war at that point. It upset me to find out what Hitler was doing in the name of Germans. And I found it confusing that we still had family back there in Germany who would be fighting for Hitler.

Now, most people if you ignore them, they shut up because it gets boring having a go at people who don't react. But not Henry. I knew he wasn't the smartest of people and I soon realized that he actually thought we'd changed our name for more sinister reasons – because we were German spies and had been since the First World War.

At first I laughed at this. Then, when he started to spread it around his pals in Kalamazoo, it annoyed me. It came to a head one day and we had a big fight. This time I was so angry, I really let him have it. As a result I got into trouble. Henry's parents complained to the school principal. Our two families stopped talking to each other. That was in 1940 when we were fifteen. Time passed. We both left school. The war overseas continued. Then, after the Japanese attack on Pearl Harbor, America joined the war.

As soon as I could, I joined up. Henry Pelt became a distant memory. One of those annoying figures from your past. And now he'd come back into it. As a marine.

Chapter 5
Henry Pelt

As soon as I was fully fit, that inevitable day came when I was called back for duty. My brief time in combat seemed so distant now that I was actually looking forward to seeing my pals. I'd persuaded Mom and Pop – and Granpop Otto and Grammy Gretel – that tearful farewells didn't go with a soldier-hero son, so they'd agreed to leave me at the station on my own to wait for the train.

I was strolling along the platform when I saw Henry Pelt. He looked bigger than ever. Very muscular. He also saw me and hesitated. I could almost see his brain ticking over, wondering what to say or whether to ignore me. I decided that, because we were both wearing the same uniform, it was ridiculous to ignore one another. So I nodded at him and simply said, 'Henry.'

He nodded back, curtly, but I could tell that the animosity was still there. It was in his eyes, the way he looked at me. We stood there in silence, waiting for the train.

Then, suddenly he sneered and said, 'Don't you find it strange, fighting your own people?'

After all these years, Henry was still playing the same stupid game. I could feel the old anger welling up in me but did my best to hide it. Instead I just shrugged and said, 'That's the first I knew we were Japanese.'

Henry scowled. 'You know what I mean. We're fighting the Nazis. *Your* people.'

'My people ain't Nazis, Henry,' I responded coolly. 'We're Germans. That ain't the same thing.' With a twinkle in my eye, I added: 'Remember, the commander of the Fifth Marines is called General Schmidt. Sounds German to me. You saying a marine commander is a Nazi?'

Henry glared at me. He was always easy to beat in an argument if it required thought.

'You think you're clever,' he snapped. 'But you don't fool me. Your family changed their name trying to pretend they're not who they are. That makes you Nazi spies in my book.'

'Which book's that, Henry?' I asked innocently. 'You taken to reading lately?'

Henry's fists clenched and I thought for a moment he was going to hit me. But he unclenched them. He wasn't that stupid. He wouldn't want to get into trouble for attacking another marine in public. Especially one who'd just come back a hero from the Marianas.

'One day,' he snarled, 'you and me are gonna settle this once and for all.'

'Suits me, Henry,' I said. 'Reading books at ten paces?'

Henry shut up and just glared at me. His brain couldn't work out an answer to that one.

Just then there was a loud whistling from the distance. Our train was on its way in. I was going back to the war, and I could once again forget about Henry Pelt.

Chapter 6
Briefing Two

In fact it was many hours before I could even begin to forget about Henry Pelt. Not only were we on the same long train journey, we also caught the same bus from the station back to camp. We didn't speak the whole trip. Nor even exchange looks.

I was trying to look calm but inside I was furious. Before, Henry's accusations had just been born out of ignorance and spite. Now, with the evidence in front of him – that I'd been in combat and nearly died for our country, America – for him to call me an 'enemy Nazi' was so stupid it made my blood boil.

I was relieved when I was finally among my old buddies again and could begin to forget Henry. It was great to see them again, especially Paddy, who looked even fitter than he did before we launched our attack on Saipan.

'Hey, John!' yelled Paddy when I walked into the barrack room. 'How ya doing, old pal? Good to see you back.'

Just the sight of him with the same old lopsided grin and the warm welcome on his face made me feel good.

'Fine, Paddy,' I said. 'Got some good old Michigan air in my lungs and loafed around eating my mom's cooking. Just what the doc ordered. What's been happening here? How's the war going at the front line?'

'Things are hotting up,' said Paddy. 'You got here just in time, something big's coming up, I know it.'

'Oh?' I asked. 'What is it?'

'Dunno,' said Paddy. 'Maybe we're gonna attack Tokyo itself. Whatever it is, it's definitely cooking. The top brass have been gathering and there've been lots of top secret meetings! I feel it in my bones, John! This is the big one!'

Paddy hadn't changed a bit despite his time in combat – the same eagerness to be in the thick of things. I grinned back at him but, to be honest, I felt a twinge of my old panic at the thought of combat. I was back – and soon I'd be out there facing the guns again.

As it turned out, Paddy was almost right. Three days later we were all summoned to a mass briefing, carried out in separate halls across the base at the same time. I guess the same briefing was going on at other camps right across the US. We all filed in, sat down and found ourselves looking at a large map on the wall in front of us. I could tell straight away it was one of the Pacific islands; it had that same sharp-angled shape that so many of them had. The island of Tinian had looked a bit like that from our Marianas briefing. Plus there were the unmistakable signs of defences marked on it.

Paddy, sitting next to me, gave me a happy wink: this meant action!

'OK, let me have your attention,' snapped the briefing officer. He tapped the map of the island with his pointer. 'This, gentlemen, is Iwo Jima! Right inside Japanese territorial waters. Eight square miles, and nearly every square inch of it hides an underground Japanese defence position. Those of you who were at the Marianas, this is more of the same. But much more. This mountain here, the highest point on the island, is called Suribachi. It's a dead volcano. Which means the sand on the beaches is the same as the sand that bogged you down on Saipan, Guam and Tinian – black volcanic ash.'

As I heard this, my heart sank. I'd only been in battle for a short while, but I'd learned that black ash is almost impossible to walk across, let alone run over at speed trying to dodge enemy fire.

'When I say it's heavily defended, believe me, I'm not joking. The beaches will be mined, have no doubt about that. Our reconnaissance planes have also spotted sections just offshore where oil drums have been tied together and are floating in the surf. Our guess is that they contain explosives which will be detonated as soon as we reach them.

'Here, here and here, where the beach ends and the island proper begins, are terraces of rock. Some of them are twelve feet high. So we can't just run our tanks up from the beach. When you get off the beach you'll find that most of the island is just rock and scrub. Very little vegetation for cover. This assault means getting across the soft sand, then climbing up these rocks, and aiming for here ...' And he tapped the outlines of the airfields. 'Two fully operational airfields and a third under construction. And those airfields, gentlemen, are why we *have* to take Iwo Jima.'

I sat there with a sense of awe at what we were expected to do. And, already, I felt the fear deep in my stomach. It was going to be like Saipan all over again. Only worse.

The briefing officer continued:

'If we're going to win this war, we have to bomb Tokyo into submission. Our problem is that the nearest air-base is in the Marianas, some fifteen hundred miles from Japan. And I don't need to tell you that a three thousand mile round trip is too far for our fighter planes. So our B-29s have been flying their bombing missions to Japan without fighter escort, and they've been hitting major interception from enemy fighter planes based here at Iwo. In other words, our bombers have been sitting ducks.

'An additional difficulty is that if any of our planes get into trouble, there is nowhere safe for them to come down. If they don't make it back to base they have to ditch in the sea. That often means the loss of both the plane and the crew.'

'See, John,' Paddy whispered to me, 'I told you this was going to be the big one!'

I could sense his excitement. This was what Paddy enjoyed: danger. For me, once again, there was just numb fear. Before Saipan there had been fear of what battle would be like. Now I'd experienced it, and been injured, I knew that the reality of battle was far worse than anything that could be imagined. The officer was talking again, and I did my best to let him have my undivided attention.

'Iwo Jima is the ace in this Pacific war,' he said firmly. 'Whoever holds it, wins. If we take this island, we can bomb Japan into submission. As long as the Japanese hang on to it, we can't. In other words, it's imperative that we capture Iwo Jima.

'OK, now for the bad news. The Japanese have had a very long time to make this island a fortress. Those of you who were in the Marianas saw what they had done there. Tunnels. Caves. Everything deep underground. We bombed them and bombed them before the attack, but they were still there, alive and kicking. We're going to do the same to Iwo, but on an even bigger scale and hope this time we can really knock them out. But our experience suggests we can't count on it being one hundred per cent successful.

'We don't know how many Japanese troops are on the island. Intelligence suggests there could be anything between twenty and forty thousand of them.'

'Wow!' whispered Paddy next to me. As the obstacles we had to face on this operation mounted up so did his excitement – and so did my nerves. I just hoped Paddy never found out how I really felt.

'I'm not going to pretend this is going to be easy,' continued the briefing officer.

You can say that again, I thought.

'You'll be up against some of the fiercest defensive fighters in the world. As we've seen already, these soldiers would rather die than surrender. They're bunkered deep inside one of the most impregnable defensive structures ever constructed. But we've got to have Iwo Jima, and if there are any men on this earth who can take it, then it's you. Because you're United States marines.'

Chapter 7
Jimmy Wilson

So it was that Christmas Day 1944 found me, along with thousands of other marines, loading out. Fifteen days later we were aboard a fleet bound for Iwo Jima.

The sea journey was a long one. Forty days. Forty days to do nothing except talk and read and talk and sleep and argue and complain. Just like soldiers all over the world, we complained about everything there was to complain about. The food. The ship. The sea. The officers. The enemy. It didn't do us any good, but it helped to pass the time.

There were a lot of new recruits in our unit. One of them, a fellow called Jimmy Wilson, the same age as myself, but who seemed to me to be a lot younger, attached himself to me and Paddy. He was from New Jersey, and I can't think what on earth made him enlist in the marines. Maybe he thought it would make him look big back home. Right now, on the way to Iwo, he just seemed small and scared all the time.

Jimmy was unusual in that he made no attempt to hide his anxiety. In fact, it was all he wanted to talk about.

Personally I tried not to encourage him. I understood fear. I'd felt it on Saipan. I was certainly feeling it now. But talking about it didn't make me feel any better. Also, it might give the other guys the idea you were some kind of coward, and that was the last thing you wanted people to think of you. Especially when you were going into combat with them.

I tried to tell Jimmy this one afternoon, when just he and I were standing on the deck of our ship, looking out over the vast empty sea. Jimmy had just finished describing how worried he felt about actually facing the Japanese guns on the beach.

'Is it really that bad, John?' he asked. 'You've been there. You've been shot. You're a hero.'

'I'm no more a hero than any other man in this outfit, Jimmy,' I said. 'I was only on

Saipan for a short while. I only got as far as the beach, and then up to the pillbox where the sniper who shot me was hiding.'

I felt such deep sympathy as I saw the worried expression on Jimmy's face. He was looking to me for some words that would make him feel better. But, deep down, I was as scared as he was. I knew, no matter how I felt myself, I had to say something to try and help him. Some sort of advice.

'Listen, when you go up that beach you don't think about being a hero,' I told him. 'You don't even think about the Japanese guns. All you think about is staying alive. And maybe getting to where you're supposed to get to. Because if you stay stuck, you're dead. If you try and go back, you're dead. So the only way to stay alive is to go forward, keep your head down and stay alert.'

'But I don't know if I'll be able to kill a Japanese soldier if I saw one face to face,' he continued, his face creased into a look of concern.

'Believe me, you'll do it,' I assured him. 'One, there ain't time to think in battle. Two, if you don't kill him he's gonna kill you. That makes it very simple.' Then, trying not to hurt his feelings too much, I added 'And a word of caution, Jimmy: it's really not a good idea to tell everyone how afraid you are. Me, I don't mind you opening up to me this way. But some of the other guys might not take too kindly to it.'

'I know,' nodded Jimmy, and he dropped his eyes unhappily. 'I said this back in boot camp and I got called a coward. I had to fight to prove I wasn't.'

'Well, you don't have to fight me,' I reassured him. 'But take my tip, keep your mouth shut. It doesn't do anyone any good to talk about being scared. We're US marines and we're here to do a job. Being scared just doesn't come into it, otherwise we might as well all pack up and go home.'

I knew my words were harsh but I was worried that Jimmy's obvious fear would feed my own. He looked crushed and I felt I had to find something encouraging to say to him.

'Remember, Jimmy, the enemy are probably scared as well.'

'Are they?' asked Jimmy. 'I hear their soldiers kill themselves rather than surrender. That don't sound to me like they're scared of dying.'

Reluctantly, I was about to tell him that I agreed, when I was saved by the wail of a siren sounding throughout the ship. This was followed by a terse announcement over the loudspeakers: 'Enemy attack! Enemy attack! All hands to battle stations!'

Chapter 8
Kamikaze

As marines on board a naval vessel, we weren't meant to take part in the ship's defensive operations. While the sailors ran to their positions, Jimmy and I looked out over the sea. Some small planes were coming towards the fleet.

The shipboard anti-aircraft guns opened up with their earsplitting chatter-chatter-chatter, peppering lines of tracer towards the incoming Japanese planes.

As they got nearer, I could make them out better. Five Zeros. Single-seater fighter-bombers. Gunfire spat from them and Jimmy and I threw ourselves down as the bullets strafed the side of our ship. It was my first time under fire since Saipan and my heart began thumping loudly. I did my best to get it under control, taking deep breaths, trying to stay calm. The worst thing I could do was to show my own fear in front of Jimmy.

I heard a plane zoom overhead. I stood up again, hauling Jimmy up with me. The deep breathing had worked. My heart had returned almost to normal. Jimmy was shaking.

'It's OK,' I assured him. 'Our boys have got them in their sights.'

And as I said this, one of the Zeros burst into flames in mid-air as our anti-aircraft gunfire hit home. There was the flash of an explosion, and then it spiralled down into the sea.

'One to us,' I murmured.

The other Zeros were whirling through the sky, guns blazing. And then, as we watched, one of the planes banked and set a course directly for one of our ships. The anti-aircraft guns opened up but the plane kept on its direct flight path. I imagined that on board they were desperately trying to aim a rocket at the oncoming plane, but before they could do so it smashed into the ship's tower. There was an almighty explosion as the plane's bomb load blew up.

I watched in horror as the ship became

an inferno of fire, more exploding ammunition adding to the carnage.

Further away, through the smoke of the burning ship, I could make out another of the Zeros making straight for another of our fleet. This time the gunners brought it down, but only just in time. The Zero spun out of control, its wings shot off, and crashed into the ocean.

The remaining two Japanese planes were shot out of the sky by a mixture of rockets and intensive anti-aircraft fire. They'd been flying straight and low, so our guys had been able to pick them off. They could have taken evasive action, but it looked obvious to me that both planes had been on a collision course at their intended targets.

I stood silently on deck in complete shock. The ship that had taken a direct hit was blazing uncontrollably. Even from a distance I could see its crew and the marines jumping and scrambling down the side into the sea. Lifeboats were also being lowered. Our own course had already been altered to head for the stricken vessel, to pick up survivors.

I heard a whimpering beside me and

became aware of Jimmy again. He looked at me, his face white, his lips trembling.

'They crashed *on purpose*!' he said. 'They flew their planes right into those ships, knowing they were killing themselves at the same time.'

I nodded. 'Kamikazes. Suicide pilots. I'd heard about them, but I've never seen them before.'

'What hope have we against men who don't care if they die!' begged Jimmy.

'A lot,' I told him firmly. 'They die once, that's it, their war is over. The Japanese are scared of us because we don't die. We keep coming at them. That's why we're going to win.'

But even as I said it, I knew that my words sounded hollow. This was our enemy. Men for whom death held no fear. These were the soldiers we would be facing when we got to Iwo Jima. This was going to be a battle with few survivors.

Chapter 9
Fight

After the kamikaze attack the situation on all the ships was tense for two days. We kept expecting the Zeros to come back in larger numbers, especially as we were nearer to Japanese waters.

However, after the third day, with no sign of further attacks, things eased off. At least, for most of us. I noticed that Jimmy Wilson still seemed as shaken up as ever. I guessed the Japanese were holding their kamikaze pilots for our arrival at Iwo Jima, along with plenty of other nasty surprises.

Our ship was now packed to the limits – as were all the others in the fleet – with the survivors from the ship that had been hit. With few places to go to escape one another, I guess it was inevitable that sooner or later trouble would rear its ugly head. It popped up for me in the shape of my pal, Paddy Riley, with a black eye.

'What happened to you?' I asked.

'I had to put some joker right,' said Paddy.

'About what?' I asked.

'About you. I overheard him mouthing off about you being a Nazi spy.'

I stared at him. 'Not Henry Pelt?'

'I don't know what his name was, I didn't give him a chance to tell me. He was one of the survivors off the ship that got hit by that kamikaze pilot. Just our luck to have a yo-yo like that transferred to us. I heard him say that you are really a German sent here to spy on us. Anyway, next thing I know the two of us are going for it.' He touched his eye tenderly. 'Man, he's tough!'

'What happened?'

'Sergeant Sykes came along, so we broke it up. But it ain't finished,' he added fiercely.

'Yes it is, Paddy,' I said.

'But you can't have him spreading lies about you being German and ...'

'I *am* German,' I said, cutting Paddy off. He looked at me in astonishment.

Briefly I explained to him about my family, about Henry and our background, our time at school and Henry's attitude towards me. When I finished, Paddy looked at me, sympathetically.

'Man, that is tough!' he said. 'To have an idiot like that on your back all the time.'

'He wasn't on my back till his ship sank,' I said ruefully. 'I guessed he'd be coming out here to Iwo. Hell, nearly every marine there is, is in this fleet. But I thought he'd just stay with his battalion on his ship and I wouldn't have to see him or talk to him or anything.' I sighed. 'Looks like I was wrong. I guess now Henry's on our ship, he's going to keep this stupid thing going.'

'Trust me, John, he won't keep it going much more,' grunted Paddy. 'Not when I finish shutting his mouth up. How can any idiot call you a Nazi after what you did on the Marianas? I'm Irish, you're German, Luigi there is Italian. We all came from somewheres else.'

'I know,' I agreed.

Although my time in the marines had convinced me that I was doing the right thing and that I shouldn't be confused by my German ancestry, it was good to hear someone else who understood and didn't think it was a problem.

'Henry is an idiot though,' I continued.

'Yeah, well, he's gonna be an idiot with a bloody nose!' snapped Paddy.

I shook my head. 'Leave it, Paddy. Thanks for standing up for me, but it's OK. I can handle Henry. I handled him all the way through school. And it won't make me feel better if you end up court-martialled for fighting with another marine.'

Reluctantly, Paddy nodded. 'OK, John. But that Pelt guy sure as hell hadn't better say anything like that again when I'm around!'

As Paddy left to go and get some treatment for his eye, my heart sank a little. It was bad enough that I was about to go into combat against an enemy who didn't care about dying, now I had my old enemy, Henry Pelt, to contend with, right here on this ship. I just hoped I wouldn't have to suffer him when we actually got to Iwo Jima.

Chapter 10
Iwo Jima

For the remainder of our time on board I avoided Henry Pelt. Now and then we saw each other, but – as we had done on the train on our way back to camp from Kalamazoo – we kept our distance and didn't even acknowledge each other. I knew he was still telling his cronies his mad theories about me being a Nazi spy, but he didn't say it to my face. Nor was he trying to spread the rumour around the whole ship any more. I'd heard that he'd wised up after running into trouble with a couple of other marines with German ancestors.

I'd been able to chat to them and we all admitted that at first it had been a little bit odd to be at war against the Germans. How were our cousins and aunts and uncles in Germany feeling about us right now? I was just glad to be out in the Pacific fighting the Japanese. It must have been tough for the guys fighting in Europe. It wasn't something I could dwell on too much, though. I was American and believed in what we were fighting for.

Every day brought us closer to Iwo Jima and every day I did my best not to think about what was waiting for us when we got there. Most of the others did the same, which was why the ship was full of guys playing cards, reading, doing loads of different things, but avoiding talking about the impending battle if they could.

Finally, we were there. Iwo Jima.

We heard the sounds of battle long before we saw the island. Our briefing officer back at camp had told us that they were intending to soften up Iwo with a major bombing campaign. Well, he was as true as his word.

The non-stop bombing of Iwo Jima by our air force had been going on for over two months – the longest and heaviest bombardment there'd ever been in the Pacific. Now our battleships were doing their bit. Iwo Jima was being pounded into rubble.

As I stood on the deck and looked towards Iwo, about two miles away, I was reminded of when we were waiting to attack Saipan. Saipan had been bombed too. Not as heavily as this, but it had been bombed. And the enemy had survived.

Iwo Jima seemed to be permanently on fire. The island's one mountainous peak, Suribachi, was shrouded in smoke as missile after missile from our battleships and cruisers hit the island.

'No one can possibly stay alive under all that,' said a voice beside me.

It was Jimmy Wilson, looking out towards the island with a stunned expression as more bombs and rockets rained down on it.

I was tempted to just keep quiet – but then I decided it was wrong to send him into battle thinking it was already won. If that happened, he was as good as dead.

'Our battleships did the same thing when we invaded Saipan,' I told him. 'They bombed the island until we didn't think there could be anything or anyone left. But when we hit the beach, the enemy was waiting for us.'

'But they say our guys have been

bombing Iwo every day for seventy days!' insisted Jimmy. I could hear the note of desperate hope in his voice. He didn't want to go on to that beach and face a live enemy shooting at him. None of us did.

As I looked at the beach on Iwo, again I remembered Saipan. The defensive fire we'd encountered. The dead marines strewn about around me as I dug into the sand. And the final shot that tore my chest open. I could feel myself sweating beneath my uniform. The fear was creeping up on me again. I hoped Jimmy hadn't noticed.

More rockets blasted into the island. More explosions and flames. The sea around us boiled with the recoil. It was like watching an island being destroyed by an earthquake or a volcano. Only this volcano was man-made by the sixteen-inch guns of our battleships and the fourteen-inch guns of the destroyers and cruisers.

'They're not answering our fire. Surely they must all be dead!' Jimmy continued.

As he spoke, there was a movement from the base of the cliffs on the island as the large Japanese guns moved in their casements, and then smoke from their muzzles and the sound of thunder rolling to us across the sea.

'DOWN!' came the shout, and we all ducked.

The next second I felt our ship rock and there was the deafening sound of a blast off our port bow.

I lifted my head and peered over the rail. The Japanese had scored a direct hit on one of our destroyers and it was on fire. As I watched I could see men leaping from it into the water. Jimmy got to his feet and looked, too, his face white.

'For dead men, those Japanese sure can fight back,' I said bitterly.

Another round was fired from the island, and this one finished the destroyer off altogether, toppling it over.

'All men below decks!' barked one of the sergeants.

I turned and headed for the hatch. Jimmy Wilson stood, still staring at the men in the water and the burning ship as if transfixed, a look of horror on his face.

'Watching won't help them,' I said, maybe a bit too sharply. Jimmy turned and looked at me, his lips trembling.

'We're going to die,' he said, the terror apparent on his face.

I took a deep breath. For his sake, and for mine, I had to keep my fear under control.

'Not necessarily,' I told him, doing my best not to let my voice shake. 'When the time comes, just keep your head down and follow orders. Come on, let's get below.'

As dawn came up the next morning, it hit me that this was it. D-Day. The sea was calm. No wind. The sky was clear of cloud. Visibility was excellent. The Japanese would be able to see us coming clearly all the way in, the whole two miles. The question was, would they try to hit us while we were still out at sea, or would they wait until we got on to the beach, when we'd be closer targets?

Breakfast had been the standard before an assault: a great helping of steak and eggs. It was a standing joke among the marines: 'The condemned man ate a hearty meal.' The sick feeling in my stomach meant I had difficulty eating. I noticed that Jimmy Wilson didn't touch his food at all.

The time for the assault had been set at 0900, H-Hour. We assembled on deck and I took in the scene. Our destroyers were sending rockets into the beaches, doing their best to clear them, ready for our landing. Marine and navy planes were also at work, attacking the island, hitting the areas beyond the beaches.

There was a flurry of activity on our ship, and on all the ships along the line. Landing craft were being lowered from the assault transports, boat teams were being assembled, amphibious tractors unloaded.

'OK, platoon! Over the side and into the boats!'

'Back in action again, John!' Paddy grinned at me. 'And no getting shot again. The army can't afford to keep giving out Purple Hearts!'

I forced a grin back at him, though inside my heart was pounding and my throat felt tight.

Along with the others, I moved towards the nets that hung down the side of the ship to the waiting landing craft. I noticed Jimmy Wilson hang back, and I went over to him.

'I don't want to die, John,' he whispered as he saw me approach.

'None of us do, son,' said a gruff voice behind me.

I turned, surprised, and found Sergeant Sykes just behind me.

'Trouble?' Sykes asked me.

I shook my head. 'No, sir.'

'Good,' said Sykes.

But I could tell he didn't believe me. One look at Jimmy, trembling, was enough for him to know what was going on. I expected him to bawl Jimmy out, to order him to the boats. But to my surprise, Sykes turned to Jimmy and spoke gently to him.

'You're scared, kid,' he said. 'We're all scared. I'm scared. Any man with a brain in his head is going to be scared, doing what we're about to do. Except for guys like Paddy Riley. They seem to get a kick out of being in dangerous spots.'

I looked at Sykes in surprise. This was the last thing I'd expected: to hear him, of all people, admit that he was scared.

'It's being scared that's kept me alive,' Sykes carried on. 'I know when to duck and hide. Dead men are no use to this

63

army. But if we don't get out there and win this war, then we're gonna have a great deal more to be scared about. Our families and our children living in a world ruled by people like Hitler and the Japanese commanders. We can't let that happen.'

With that Sykes clapped Jimmy on the shoulder. 'Remember what I said,' he said. 'Keep your head down and follow orders. You'll be OK.'

Then he moved to the rail where the rest of our platoon was clambering down to the landing craft.

I looked after him, astonished. Sergeant Sykes admitting he was scared? He was one of the bravest soldiers I'd ever known. It was ironic: what Sykes had said had been for Jimmy's benefit, but it was me who felt better. If Sykes could cope with his fear, then so could I.

'Come on, Jimmy,' I said. 'Let's go. Like Sykes says, we've got a war to win.'

I headed for the rail where Paddy was waiting for me. Jimmy reluctantly followed.

'Come on, John!' Paddy called cheerfully. 'We don't want to miss this one!'

I wondered if anything ever scared

Paddy. Could he even understand what the rest of us were going through?

We climbed down the net into the boat and joined the rest of our platoon. The small landing vehicle rocked from side to side in the sea.

This was it. We were on our way to face the enemy.

Chapter 11
Landing

Rockets and missiles from our battleships and destroyers were still pounding the island, the barrage continuing non-stop. I could see the reconnaissance planes flying over Iwo, radioing the positions of the Japanese defences back to the battleships to help them pinpoint their targets. As I watched, the battleships moved in closer to the island to see if they could knock out the pillboxes and blockhouses.

'That sure is some fancy shooting!' muttered a marine near me, admiringly, as shell after shell from the *Arkansas* smashed into the Japanese defences. 'Hope they leave something standing for me to take. I promised to win me a medal to take home for my pa.'

'OK, men!' hollered Sergeant Sykes. 'We're go!'

Our assault craft moved away from our mother ship. Luckily the sea was calm, so it didn't rock too much. Ahead of us were a wave of amphibious tractors armed with 75 mm howitzers and machine-guns. In theory they would clear a path for us on to the beach by keeping up a steady fire at everything in their way.

After us would come the LSMs bringing the tanks and bulldozers. Once the marines were on shore and moving in, the final section of this first wave would land, the corpsmen and Seabees.

I knew in my gut that it was going to be Saipan all over again. It was going to be hard, bloody and messy.

So far, however, there had been no firing from the island. No defensive rockets, no small arms fire. Nothing. The enemy were waiting and holding their fire.

We all crouched down in our LVT. My guts felt like they were twisted and my hands sweated as I gripped my rifle.

I thought about what Sergeant Sykes had said. He was scared. I was scared. We all were scared. Except Paddy Riley. I turned and looked at Paddy, who was squatting next to me. He gave me a wink.

Then I turned and looked at Jimmy Wilson. His face was whiter than ever and his lips moved as if in silent prayer. He didn't look at me, he didn't look at anyone or anything. I could tell he was absolutely terrified.

'It'll be OK,' I whispered encouragingly to him. But he didn't respond. He was lost inside his own fear.

As we neared the beach there was a roaring noise from overhead. I looked up and there above us were a force of B-29 bombers, heading for Iwo. As we watched, bombs rained down and filled the morning sky with smoke and explosions. Following the B-29s came the dive-bombers, once again pinpointing pillboxes and blockhouses.

By now we were almost at the shore. The waves were breaking over our LVT. Ahead of us, the armoured amphtracs had reached the beach and begun climbing out of the surf on to the black volcanic sand. Still there had been no fire from the Japanese positions.

'Maybe they're all dead,' murmured someone.

'Don't bet your life on it,' replied his buddy.

It was as our LVT rode in on the surf that the Japanese defences finally opened up with mortar and artillery shells. The water around our craft shot up in columns as mortars crashed around us. To our starboard side, another LVT took a direct hit. The two dozen men in it tumbled into the water. Some of them were already dead and just sank. The injured did their best to keep afloat, but the weight of their full packs pulled them down beneath the surface of the water.

I turned my eyes away from the scene and concentrated on the beach that was fast approaching. More explosions around us. More columns of water crashing down on us. Our craft lurched slightly as the caterpillar tracks bit into the loose sand beneath the waves. Then we were coming up out of the surf, trundling on to land. We'd made it. We were on Iwo Jima.

Smoke from US bomb hits trails over Iwo Jima.

Landing craft advance towards the beaches of Iwo Jima.

US Marines storm ashore at Iwo Jima.

US Marines clear Japanese soldiers from caves on Mount Suribachi.

Japanese pillbox blasted by US navy bombardment.

US Marines probe mines on Iwo Jima to clear a path for vehicles.

US Marines weighed down with flame throwers move inland.

An injured US Marine is helped away from the
fighting lines.

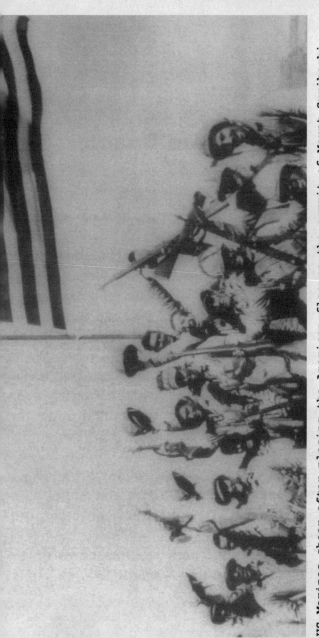

US Marines cheer after placing the American flag on the summit of Mount Suribachi.

Chapter 12
On the Beach

'Keep your heads down!' shouted Sergeant Sykes.

Those of us who'd been in combat before didn't need to be told, we were already crouched down. This was where many a novice met his end, peering up at the beach from over the rim of an LVT and giving a sniper a target.

Now that we'd made land, the Japanese defences opened up with a vengeance. Mortars and artillery fire rained down on us, bullets ricocheting off our armoured plating.

'OK!' shouted Sykes, raising his voice so he could be heard above the sounds of gunfire. 'Let's get off this thing! Hit the beach!'

The landing ramp crashed down on to the black sand and, keeping low, we broke into a stampede for the nearest ridge. I threw myself down face first into the soft sand. Paddy was next to me. Bullets whizzed over our heads, still clanging off the armour of the LVT.

I rolled over and looked behind me for Jimmy Wilson. He was still crouched in the amphtrac, his face petrified.

'Get outa there, marine!' bellowed Sykes. 'Get outa there before they kill you!'

Jimmy slowly forced himself up and began to run forward, his boots clanging on the metal of the ramp. As he reached the sand he suddenly stopped, spun round and crumpled. Even from where I was I could see the blood on the pale skin of his neck.

'JIMMY!' I shouted.

I felt sick. This was my fault. I knew how scared he was. Somehow I was managing to control my own fear but I should have realized that Jimmy just couldn't do it.

My mind raced wildly. I should have told him to go to the company doctor. Pretend to be sick. But no, I knew that wouldn't have worked. The doc would have just given him some pills and kicked him out. If Jimmy had told the truth – that he was too scared to go into combat – he would have been thrown in the brig and then sent back in disgrace. Would he have been able to stand that? Suddenly, all Sykes's words of advice to Jimmy seemed hollow. Jimmy had followed orders, he'd gone into battle, and he'd been shot.

Then it hit me – no, I was wrong. Jimmy *hadn't* followed orders. Jimmy had stayed behind on the amphtrac and so given an enemy sniper time to get a good aim at him. If he'd followed Sykes's orders he would have been up here on the beach with the rest of us, right now, in cover behind this sand ridge.

I'd been lost in my own thoughts, but suddenly I realized that Jimmy was moving. He hadn't been killed, just wounded.

'Hang on, Jimmy!' I shouted. 'Stay low, you'll be OK.'

I was relieved. Jimmy would be picked up by the corpsmen, taken back to the ships and tucked up nicely. He could sit out the rest of the war with a Purple Heart, a war hero, wounded at Iwo Jima.

It was an ironic thought. It was almost what had happened to me back at Saipan.

Shot in the first few minutes of the landing. This time on Iwo Jima I was facing a real test. Could I go all the way?

Tug Reed, our radio operator, was speaking into his mike, reporting our situation back to the ships:

'Fox Company, 28th Division, landed on Green Beach safely. Limited casualties, but coming under heavy fire now. Over.'

There was a crackling from his radio set as our base responded. I couldn't make out what they were saying – for that you needed a radio operator's ears, trained over years so that they could make out what people were saying through radio hiss and static – but from his reply I guessed they were asking what sort of fire we were coming under.

'Mainly small arms fire. Machine-guns,' reported Tug.

A huge explosion just ahead of us shook the ground beneath me and sand and rocks rained down on us.

Tug shook the sand off him, spat some sand out, and added into his mike: 'Also mortar fire. Over.'

Behind this ridge, we were also in the cover of the first terrace of rock, which was about three feet high. It didn't give us much protection, just enough to make it difficult for the machine-gunners and snipers to get a bead on us. Because of this, the Japanese had started using mortars against us.

Ahead of us I knew there was a pillbox. I'd spotted it as we came in to land. Low, squat, with a narrow opening in its concrete face, half-buried in sand and rock for camouflage, it had somehow survived the intensive bombing. It was Saipan all over again – trapped on a beach, held down by gunfire from a concealed pillbox. Back then I'd tried to knock it out, and had got shot for my pains.

'OK, you guys,' said Sykes. 'We gotta take that pillbox out or else we can't move off this beach. It's no use radioing for rockets from the ships to knock it out. For one thing, it's set too low down. Also, at this range, our ships are just as likely to hit us.'

Almost as if it was someone else's voice speaking, I heard myself say: 'I'll do it, sarge.'

I had to know if I could get a handle on my fear and do what was right. My own life and the lives of my fellow marines depended on it.

'You don't go without me,' grunted a voice beside me. It was Paddy.

Sykes looked at me quizzically.

'You sure about this, Smith?' he asked. 'Last time you tried this you got badly shot up.'

'Maybe this time I get the chance to do it right,' I said wryly.

It sounded brave, but deep down I didn't feel it. I still remembered the fear I'd felt when I'd gone up to the pillbox on Saipan. The rifle poking out at me. I'd be facing that again, but if I didn't, I knew I'd never be able to get past it. It was something I had to do.

Sykes nodded. 'OK, which way will you go up?'

I did my best to remember how the pillbox was sited. If my observation had been correct, it jutted out from an overhang of rock. That was part of its camouflage. I hoped the rock would give me some cover.

'There's a body of rock to the right of it,' I said. 'If I can get up that way, with luck I might be able to get a couple of grenades through the opening.'

'I'll be right behind you, gun ready,' said Paddy. 'If I see any rifle barrels poking out at you, I'm gonna let them have it, so get ready to dive for the ground when I shout.'

'Good,' said Sykes. 'In that case I'll take some men up towards the left, keep 'em busy with a decoy action.' He shouted along the line: 'Redmond, di Maggio, Anderson! You're with me!'

With that, Sykes began crawling along the beach, using the ridge of sand and the terrace of rock behind it as cover. Redmond, di Maggio and Anderson followed him, moving jerkily forward on their knees and elbows, guns at the ready.

I looked at Paddy.

'Looks like us again,' I forced a grin.

'You sure you're ready for this?' asked Paddy quietly. I suddenly realized that, despite his own apparent lack of fear, he knew exactly how I felt. He knew that I was thinking of Saipan and he knew that I was scared.

'I can do this and you can be my cover,' he suggested.

I shook my head. 'No, this one's mine. Let's do it.'

Chapter 13
Pillbox

Paddy and I set off, me in front, Paddy close behind, crawling fast and low, digging into the soft sand with our knees and elbows. When we reached the point where I guessed the rock overhang began, I stopped. I slung my gun over a shoulder and pulled two grenades out.

I looked back at Paddy, checking he was ready. He nodded. All we could do now was wait for Sykes and his decoy crew to open up. We only had to wait a few moments. There was the sound of gunfire from further along the beach, round towards the left. Then the enemy soldiers in the pillbox opened up, their fire aimed towards the decoys. That was my signal.

I hauled myself up from behind the ridge and rolled at speed over the soft sand towards the terrace of rock. To my left the firing continued, Sykes and the boys making it look like a real attack. Now I was in action, there was no time to be scared. I moved instinctively, almost without thought.

I knelt and popped my head up to peer over the terrace. I could see the pillbox above me in the rock, but I couldn't see any rifle barrels. The concrete was so thick that they could fire from deep within. I hoped that such a thick layer of concrete meant they'd be restricted to firing dead ahead, or side to side, and that they couldn't swing their guns at me so easily.

I hauled myself up over the terrace of rock. The opening of the pillbox was just about fifty feet away. Because the opening was so narrow I couldn't afford to take the chance of throwing the grenades and hoping I'd get them in. If I missed it would give away our position, and both Paddy and I would get gunned down for sure. I had to get close enough to pop them in. I gripped the grenades tightly with one hand, leaving the other free to help me make it up the slope.

Here goes nothing! I thought. And then I was scrambling up the rock as fast as I could, my fingers tearing at the thin scrub covering it to try to get a handhold. The fire from Sykes and the others carried on, hammering away at the Japanese position, holding their attention, I hoped ... Fifty feet, forty feet, thirty, getting closer ... Twenty, ten ...

As if in a slow-motion dream, I tore the pin from the first grenade, and then the second. One, two, three ... and I tossed both in through the narrow slit. Then I let myself fall back down the slope, nearly crashing into Paddy.

There was a muffled BOOM from above and smoke billowed out from the pillbox. Paddy and I hit the black sand and both lay there for a second, waiting for gunfire from above, but it never came. The firing from the other side of the pillbox had also stopped. I was still wiping smoke from my eyes when Sykes and the boys appeared. Sykes was grinning broadly.

'Well done, Smith!' he smiled. 'Our way up is clear, at least as far as that pillbox. Let's get this island taken!'

*

With the pillbox above us out of action, our platoon could now scramble up to higher ground. We still bent low all the time, keeping to the cover of rocks as much as we could, because we didn't know where the next Japanese hiding-place might be.

From our new position I turned and looked back at the beach. I could see that Jimmy Wilson had managed to drag himself to cover and been able to tie something around his neck, so I guessed – and hoped – his wound had just been a flesh one. I was glad that for him the war was over.

Elsewhere along the beach other marines were coming under heavy fire. Casualties were strewn around. Some hadn't even made it to the beach and floated in the surf. Others lay where they had fallen, half covered by sand, or draped over rocks. It seemed our platoon had been fairly lucky.

We had been briefed on the voyage out to Iwo and the strategy was that each battalion had responsibility for a five hundred yard stretch of beach. Our battalion's stretch was on the west beach.

Our assignment was to go up from the beach and sweep round the northern base of Mount Suribachi to seal it from the rest of the island.

The other battalions had their own tasks: the 27th was to move west from Red Beach and follow us, then break off and head due north. The 23rd on Yellow Beach was the battalion nearest to Number One Airfield. Their job was to get on to the airfield and take it. Then they were also to head north. The 25th, meanwhile, coming ashore on Blue Beach, would head inland to link up with the other battalions and join in the chase due north.

Our first job was to establish a beach-head. We had to secure the beach for the next wave: the LSMs that carried the tanks and bulldozers. After them would come the LCVPs: ramp boats with half-tracks, anti-tank guns and Jeeps. With them came support personnel to take over the beaches after we'd moved on.

Once they hit the beaches the technical stuff started to be put together: like laying the wire matting so that vehicles could make their way over the soft sand, and establishing radio bases.

All this was the great invasion plan and in the briefing sessions on board ship it had looked great. But a plan on paper and a combat assault in practice are two different things, as I knew from my short experience at Saipan. For one thing, the soft sand here was even more treacherous than in the Marianas. Looking back down at the beach I could see that the trucks that had managed to get ashore were having trouble. Many of them were bogged down, stuck to halfway up their wheel hubs in it.

Many of the half-tracks and tanks were still down on the beach, unable to get up between the rocky terraces because the ground was so steep. I watched them as they moved backwards and forwards along the beach, looking for a way up, while enemy shells burst around them. Further out, some of the landing-craft were stuck in the surf and vulnerable to Japanese fire. Men were dropping like flies as they came under the barrage of enemy guns.

'Would you look at that,' said Paddy, who was also looking down at the chaos and carnage on the beach. 'Those poor guys,' he continued in an unusually sombre voice. 'We're lucky we made it this far.'

I agreed with Paddy, we had been lucky – but the enemy was still firmly entrenched in their bunkers and we had no choice but to move forward to face them.

Chapter 14

Under Fire

For the next hour we just stayed where we were, keeping our heads down and letting the enemy fire over us. Mortars dropped behind us, spraying shrapnel in all directions. Our ships continued to send rockets and missiles into the Japanese positions on the island. Grimly I weighed up the possibility that, with us in the middle of all this heavy cross-fire, our chances of getting hit were very high. However, I did my best to push that thought to the back of my mind. This was no time to let my fear take hold of me. I kept reminding myself of Jimmy Wilson when that had happened to him.

By late afternoon our platoon had scrambled and clawed its way up the rock-face of the terraces. Behind and below us the fighting on the beach continued. The supply amphtracs struggled out of the sea on to the beach under constant enemy fire, bringing with them medical supplies and ammunition. And more and more men. The ship-to-shore line was opening up slowly, and taking heavy casualties.

On our way up the terraces we came upon another half-dozen Japanese pillboxes and bunkers. Three of them had been flattened by our intensive bombing into smashed concrete. The others were still in action.

This time other volunteers took on the job of knocking out the first two, both times with grenades through a slit. The third one was a tougher nut to crack. The Japanese inside it kept up a constant volley of fire, pinning us down. There was no way we could get near it.

Sergeant Sykes crawled over to Redmond, who had the flame-thrower.

'You any good with that thing, Redmond?' he asked.

'I can burn a fly at fifteen feet, sarge,' cracked Redmond.

'Forget cooking insects,' snapped Sykes. 'You think you can take out that pillbox under fire?'

'Only one way to find out,' grinned Redmond.

He crawled along the low ridge of rock that gave us cover from the marksmen in the pillbox. Cautiously he peered over the ridge, then ducked his head down again. He looked over at Sykes and nodded.

'Reckon it's worth a try,' he said. 'I'll give 'em a burst from behind here, just to keep 'em back. Get ready to start firing if they come out.'

Sykes nodded. We cocked our rifles.

Redmond lay on his back in an awkward position, the heavy flame-thrower held in his powerful hands aimed over his head in the general direction of the concrete Japanese pillbox. There was an explosion, then a sudden roar and a belch of flame burst out, filling the air. Next, Redmond was up on his feet, the long flame roaring away, now covering the narrow slit in the pillbox. The firing from the pillbox stopped abruptly and I saw two men stumbling out, smoke coming from their uniforms. They turned and aimed their guns at us, but before they could fire a hail of bullets from our platoon cut them down.

Redmond switched off the flame-thrower.

'OK,' ordered Sykes grimly. 'On we go.'

I closed my eyes for a moment and shuddered at the thought of what a weapon like that could do. But then I forced that thought to the back of my mind. This was war, and war called for extreme measures.

We dragged ourselves up over the final ridge and found we were on a plateau stretching north. About a mile from our position, runways, heavily damaged, now mostly craters in places, criss-crossed it. We'd made it to the edge of Airfield One! Dotted across it were many bunkers and underground defensive positions.

'Right, men,' said Sykes, looking up at the sky, 'this is where we dig in. Remember, our objective isn't the airfield: our assignment is Mount Suribachi.'

We all looked up at the mountain towering above us. It appeared to be even more heavily fortified than the airfield. Up there were yet more Japanese positions, with the tactical advantage of higher ground.

From all over the island I could hear the sounds of battle as the other marine battalions met fierce resistance from the Japanese defenders. Even though the ships had stopped firing there was the constant noise of mortars and rockets being launched and exploding, and the never-ending, ear-splitting chatter-chatter-chatter of small-arms fire hammering out.

My feelings of fear were beginning to be replaced by extreme tiredness. I wasn't the only one. A look at the faces of the guys around me showed they all felt as exhausted as I did. Sykes was right to dig in at this stage. Worn down and battle-weary as we were, to have attempted an assault on the lower defences of Mount Suribachi would have been suicidal. With darkness beginning to fall, if we didn't get mown down by hidden machine-guns, we'd break our ankles in the potholes in the rocks.

To make sure we were protected against enemy gunfire, we took out our spades and began to dig foxholes for the night. We piled rocks around them for added protection. After that, all we could do was slide down into our foxholes and try to grab some sleep.

Darkness fell quickly, as it always does in the tropics. One minute it's daylight, then there's a funny weird kind of light, and then it's pitch black. It would have been the same here on Iwo except that the night air was filled with the glare of explosions from both sides. Powerful searchlights from our ships out at sea also lit up the darkness. They were looking for targets high on Mount Suribachi, still intent on pounding it into submission. Rockets fired from the ships powered over our heads and smashed into the mountain, shaking the ground beneath us.

The ships also sent up star shells. These exploded in mid-air and descended slowly on parachutes, giving off a bright-yellow light, to show up any movement by the Japanese. What with all the noise and the lights, by the time dawn rose on D-Day plus one, most of us hadn't slept a wink. I hoped the Japanese had been kept awake as well. I didn't relish the thought of going up against an enemy who not only knew every nook and cranny of this island, but was more alert than I was.

As the sun rose there was a lull in the

noise and I felt my eyelids drooping. At last, I thought, I'm going to get some sleep.

'OK, you guys,' snapped Sykes's voice, 'let's go!'

Chapter 15
Pinned Down

In fact we didn't go anywhere straight away. As we rose from our foxholes, ready to move towards the path to Mount Suribachi, a volley of fire opened up from the Japanese positions there, and it kept coming. Machine-guns, mortars, rifles, everything rained down on us.

We quickly slid back into our foxholes. Sykes told Tug Reed to get on the RT and get some rockets blasting into the mountain.

'And tell them to start hitting it quick! And remind them that we're here as well!' snapped Sykes. 'We want them bombing the Japanese, not us!'

We had marked our positions with white cloth panels to identify us to our own side, so they wouldn't bomb us in error. But mistakes had been known to happen.

From my position I could look down on the beach far below and see the result of the first day of our attack. It was a mess. For the whole two miles of its length, junk lay on the black sand or bobbed about in the surf – packs, blankets, rifles, gas masks and personal articles, plus the shattered and twisted amphtracs, Jeeps, tanks and landing-craft, half in, half out of the water.

Many of the heavy machines brought ashore to make the roadways had been hit and lay there, useless. Worse than useless, because, along with all the other wreckage, they formed a barrier which prevented the incoming vessels from finding a place to land.

Now, with dawn, the evacuation of casualties was taking place. The thought that those poor men had lain out on the beach all night horrified me. I just hoped that Jimmy had made it. About a mile offshore were a bunch of LSTs, obviously doubling as temporary hospital ships. The real hospital ships were further out, with the rest of the fleet. As I watched, corpsmen were at work, loading the wounded on to the amphtracs and ferrying them out to the LSTs. All the time they were under Japanese fire.

A sudden fierce explosion from Mount Suribachi shook the ground around us, then another. Our ships were pounding the Japanese positions, just as Sykes had asked.

'OK!' yelled Sykes. 'GO GO GO!'

Over the ridge we went and then, crouching low, ran for the next available shelter, which was a heap of rocks and boulders near by.

The shelling from our ships only gave us momentary cover. The Japanese deep inside their mountain bunkers opened fire. I saw Di Maggio throw up his arms and collapse. Then I was diving and rolling, ignoring the pain as my body hit small rocks, rolling into the cover of the larger boulders.

We regrouped and took stock. In that run of about fifty yards, we'd lost three men – Di Maggio, Compton and Vidor. Their bodies lay sprawled out on the open scrub, Japanese bullets still picking at them. Sykes grabbed the RT mike from Tug Reed and hollered into it: 'Fox Company coming under heavy fire. Pinned down at base of Suribachi. Increase bombardment of Japanese positions so we can get going!'

For the next hour the bombardment from our ships kept up, hammering the enemy positions. It didn't seem to have a lot of effect. Now and then there was a lull in their firing, but then it started up again. I guess the enemy had got used to being shelled this way; they'd endured nearly three months of it and weren't going to give up now.

All we could do was crouch and wait. Now and then we'd take a potshot at the Japanese positions above us, but it was of little use: they were too deeply entrenched. Tug began getting radio reports about the situation elsewhere. Apparently, on the other side of the airfield, the other companies were having the same problem as we were: deeply entrenched Japanese defences keeping them down with constant fire raking across the open ground.

What was worse was that the Japanese high on Suribachi had a perfect view of the airfield itself. Not just the airfield, but the whole island. While they held the mountain stronghold, this invasion wasn't going anywhere.

'There's gotta be some way we can get them outa there!' snarled Paddy.

'Listen up!' called Sykes. 'We're just gonna have to do this inch by inch. I'm gonna call for more bombing. Real saturation. Air strikes. When it happens we're gonna make for that path over there.'

The path he was talking about was the main approach to the mountain. A narrow rocky track, it was about 1,300 yards long and roughly 200 yards from our present position.

'Stay off the path itself! It's sure to be mined!' Sykes reminded us. 'Keep in cover either side of it. The nearer we can get to the base of the mountain, the harder it'll be for the enemy to fire down at us. Remember, they're dug in deep. OK? On my signal, because when the bombing starts you ain't gonna hear me calling, that's for sure.'

With that, Sykes gave the thumbs up to Tug Reed, who got on to the RT to give our position and the Japanese positions, as well as calling for air strikes. Our bombers arrived swiftly, coming in from the aircraft-carriers, dodging the anti-aircraft flak, turning over the northern end of the island before zooming back in and letting their loads hammer into the mountain.

BOOM! BOOM! BOOOM! BOOOMMM!

Bomb after bomb smashed into the ground, sending up clouds of dust and smoke as if the extinct volcano had come alive again. Amid all this, I looked towards Sykes and saw him leap up and wave his arm, pointing to where the mountain path was. This was it. Our only chance. I hurled myself out from behind the large rock, rifle at the ready, and ran as fast as I could, dodging and weaving to confuse snipers.

There was an explosion near me and I half turned, in time to see Redmond being hurled into the air. He'd trodden on a mine. I turned and rushed over to him as he lay, flopped on the earth. He was bleeding badly.

'Idiot!' he muttered, his voice muffled with blood. Then he went limp. He was dead.

Chapter 16
Mount Suribachi

I looked ahead. Sykes, Paddy and the rest of the platoon had found cover of a sort in rocks and bushes, not far from the narrow path up to the mountain. I picked the flame-thrower off the ground and hurried over to join them.

'Redmond's dead,' I reported. 'Mine.'

Sykes nodded. 'No more rushing. Before you move, keep your eyes peeled.'

He looked at the base of the mountain through his field-glasses. I turned to look back at the way we had come. Our reserves were moving up to join us, despite the constant fire from the Japanese.

It was now the middle of the afternoon. Hours had passed and we'd only covered a few hundred yards. During that time the marines had been launching a steady attack on Airfield One. Tanks had made it up from the beach and were advancing across the plateau, marines following them.

Despite shelling from the enemy positions on the mountain, the marines on the airfield were doing a good job, clearing out the pillboxes and bunkers.

Sykes put down his field-glasses.

'OK,' he said, 'I've got the picture. There are caves at the foot of the mountain, near where this path ends. We know the Japanese have been digging tunnels. My guess is that they've used natural tunnels inside the mountain to link their bunkers and pillboxes. Tunnels probably lead from those caves into their system. If we can't flush 'em out from outside, we've got to go in and flush 'em out from inside.'

What Sykes said made sense. Lava flows had riddled the volcano with channels. The Japanese had been on Iwo for years. It was perfect defensive strategy to expand those channels into a network of usable tunnels. Obviously that was how they'd been able to withstand our bombardment for so long, day after day, night after night – by living deep underground. When one bunker came under heavy attack, they just moved through the tunnels to another, like ants working their way through an anthill.

'OK,' said Sykes, 'there's no way we can get up that path in daylight. What we're gonna do is sit tight here. When it gets dark, we make for the caves. Once in them, we split up into pairs and work our way up. Clear?'

We nodded. But once again I could feel the fear rising up in me. We were going into unknown territory. Into caves inside the mountain, where we'd be meeting the enemy face to face. Hand to hand. Fighting to the death.

'Right,' said Sykes, 'bunker down. Grab some shut-eye. You're gonna need it. Smith, you and Riley take first watch.'

I was relieved to take first watch. The images of what was waiting for us inside those caves would have kept me from sleeping anyway, no matter how tired I was. So we settled down to wait for nightfall. And with it came the rain.

After the tropical heat of the day, we hadn't expected it. And it didn't just rain, it poured down, so thick you could hardly see through it – a curtain of water falling down. And it was cold. The previous night had been cold, too, but this was much worse. Anyone who thinks a night on a Pacific island is going to be paradise ought to spend it outside in freezing rain in a foxhole rapidly turning to mud.

At 0400 we were ready to move and soaking wet.

'This is worse than when I went to see my grammy's home in Ireland,' grunted Paddy. 'And believe me, you think it rains in Kalamazoo, that ain't nothing to the rain in Ireland.'

'I guess that's why they call it the Emerald Isle,' I commented. 'All that rain makes the grass grow so green.'

'You better believe it,' said Paddy. 'But at least Irish rain is warm. They call it soft. This stuff is freezing and hard. I don't envy the Japanese who've been living on this rock.'

'They're lucky, they've been living underground,' I pointed out.

Our foxhole was now a small pond. The sides were slippery mud.

'OK!' called Sykes. 'Get ready to move out! Keep low, keep slow, keep quiet. And thank God for this rain, it'll give us extra cover.'

'It'll give me pneumonia,' Paddy complained. 'All this way, battle after battle, and I'll finally die of pneumonia.'

Under cover of the darkness and the rain we moved forward, slowly, watching for the glint of metal that might be the tell-tale sign of a mine. From above us came the sound of firing from the Japanese, but their shots went wide or over our heads. They were firing blind, just trying to keep us down.

We stuck to the edges of the narrow path, keeping to where it was rocky and therefore not so easy to place a mine. Again, I felt a tightness on my chest and a sick feeling in my stomach. One false step and BOOOM! I took deep breaths and forced myself to think of other things. Positive thoughts. We were going to win this war. But all the time I kept my eyes peeled, scouring the ground in front of me before I put my foot down.

The sky would light up as our ships launched star shells and we'd throw ourselves down, out of sight of the Japanese. Then we'd stumble up and carry on, getting nearer yard by yard to the foot of the old volcano and the heart of the Japanese defences.

At last, after what seemed like hours, we made it. We staggered out of the drenching rain into the cover of a cave. It was great to be out of the rain, but it felt weird to be inside the mountain, inside the Japanese defences. It suddenly occurred to me that if our own ships and planes carried on bombing Mount Suribachi, we could become casualties of our own side. But then I remembered that the Japanese had survived this long by staying underground.

'OK,' said Sykes, 'let's see what we've got here.'

He took out his torch and shone it around the walls of the cave. Here, in this outer cave, was just rock. But we could see dark patches in the torchlight where tunnels extended deeper into the mountain. 'OK,' whispered Sykes, 'this is where we split up. Two to a tunnel.' He gestured at us, pairing us off. Paddy and I, as so often before, were teamed up.

Sykes took a look at Redmond's flame-thrower in my hands.

'Seeing as you've got it, you might as well keep it,' he said.

'No problem, sarge,' I nodded.

'Right,' he said, 'let's hit them from where they ain't expecting it. Let's go!'

Chapter 17

Inside the Volcano

Paddy and I crept into our assigned tunnel. I went first, the flame-thrower a dead weight on my arms, the pack with the gasoline an even heavier weight on my back. I couldn't help but be impressed by the engineering feat the Japanese had carried out here. Along the walls ran electricity supply cables, pipes for running water, even pipes that were hot. I guessed they contained steam to keep them warm below ground.

'Man!' whispered Paddy behind me. 'They got a whole city inside here!'

We moved carefully, straining our ears for any sounds of movement ahead. Above us, we heard the familiar chatter-chatter-chatter of machine-gun fire. Outside dawn must have broken and the Japanese had begun their deadly fire across the open ground of the airfield and the path that led to the foot of the mountain.

We headed towards the sound of gunfire. I cradled the flame-thrower, finger on the trigger, barrel pointing straight ahead. A faint light ahead stopped us in our tracks. We edged forward. A side tunnel led off into a large cave with rooms hollowed out of it.

'It's a hospital!' I gasped in amazement. Complete with beds, surgical instruments, medical equipment, all deep underground. No wonder the Japanese had survived for so long.

There was a sound from the entrance to the hospital cave. Spinning round, we came face to face with a Japanese soldier. He gaped at us, astonished to find us there. And then his hand reached for the pistol in his belt. Paddy let off a burst from his rifle that took the Japanese in the chest before he could get his weapon out.

As the dead soldier slumped to the ground, we moved quickly back out into the main tunnel. The shots echoed loudly in the cave. I just hoped that, with all the firing going on elsewhere, the Japanese wouldn't think anything unusual was happening.

We hurried along with the sound of firing getting louder. A pillbox was in the rock just ahead of us. I motioned Paddy to stay back. I stepped forward into its entrance, the flame-thrower poised. I just had time to see the backs of the Japanese snipers, and one turning towards me, surprise on his face, before I pressed the trigger, turning the muzzle of the flame-thrower through an arc as I did so. The flames filled the pillbox. It was over in seconds. One less Japanese defensive position.

On we went, always moving upwards, inside the extinct volcano. I was soaked in sweat. It wasn't just the weight of the flame-thrower, it was the fear that was with me, just beneath the surface. I fought it off. If I let it take over, I knew I would panic and run. I had to go on. We *had* to take this island.

Another small tunnel appeared just ahead of us, with more deafening firing echoing from it. Another pillbox. I was moving forward towards the entrance when a Japanese soldier came out. He didn't hesitate, a reflex reaction brought his rifle up and he fired. I felt the bullets pass by me and thud into Paddy just behind me. Paddy yelled and I heard him crash to the rocky floor. I didn't look round, my finger was already pressing the trigger of the flame-thrower.

Wasting no more time, I raced round the corner into the entrance of the pillbox, just as the remaining Japanese soldier was turning to face me, his gun at the ready.

Another roar of belching flame and he too was finished.

I ran back to check on Paddy. He was alive but the bullets had badly damaged his left arm. Blood was pumping out from his ripped uniform.

'I'll go get help,' I told him.

Paddy forced a grin.

'Where from?' he asked, fighting back the pain. 'No, go on and finish the job. I've got my right arm. I can hold a gun. I've still got my legs. I'll see if I can make it back to that hospital cave, fix myself up.'

'With one arm?' I said. 'We'll get you back to the hospital cave together. I'll fix you up.'

Paddy started to protest, but I shut him

up. We both knew that if he stayed here, or tried to fix his arm himself, he'd probably bleed to death. I fixed a crude tourniquet around the top of his shattered arm. Then we headed back down the tunnel, me taking point, the flame-thrower at the ready, Paddy stumbling along behind.

We were in luck. We didn't meet anyone on the way back to the hospital cave. Once there I set to work, first giving Paddy painkillers to dull the agony, and then strapping and bandaging his arm as best I could.

Even with the painkillers, I could tell Paddy was in agony. Luckily for us no Japanese came in while I worked on him. I guessed they were too busy manning their defensive positions.

I'd just finished tying Paddy's arm across his chest and fixing it in position with a bandage, when a sudden explosion shook us and pieces of rock began to fall down from the ceiling of the hospital cave. The roof was collapsing!

Chapter 18
Rescue

It felt like the whole mountain was coming down on top of us. We ran and stumbled along the tunnels, heading downwards to what we hoped was the outside. Blinded by dust, Paddy and I crashed into the rock walls. Fear drove us on faster and faster. I was terrified that if I didn't get out I'd be buried here under tons of rocks.

Obviously our fleet had begun pounding the volcano again, trying to drive the Japanese out or to crush them, and they'd scored a direct hit on the area above the hospital cave.

By some miracle, stumbling along as we did like two blind mice, we suddenly felt a gush of cold air on our faces and saw faint light through the dust.

'THIS WAY!' I shouted to Paddy.

We made for the light and soon we were

outside, desperately taking in great lungfuls of clean, dust-free air.

The mountain shook again and again as more missiles smashed into it. Then the pounding stopped. All I had was a ringing in my ears. Through it I could hear the familiar sounds of rifles and machine-guns. Out here, in the open air, the battle for Iwo Jima was still going on.

Paddy and I took cover back in the entrance to the cave. Paddy slumped down against a rock, where he could at least lie comfortably. I took a quick look around, checking the surrounding area. There was no sign of Sergeant Sykes or the rest of our platoon. I guessed they were still inside the mountain.

I looked along the narrow path to the airfield. Marines were taking cover alongside it. I let off a burst of rifle fire at the path, scattering dirt in the air. There was an explosion as I hit one of the buried mines. I looked across at one of the marines. I made out a thumbs-up sign from him to say thanks for the warning about the mines.

Here, at the foot of the mountain, I had

a good view over the airfield, and my heart gave a leap. US tanks were firmly in place, providing cover for more marines to swarm on to it. It looked as if the airfield had been taken! We were winning!

One of the marines down the path was talking into his RT and in response a tank appeared, lumbering up from the airfield. The Japanese above us on Suribachi opened fire, but their bullets bounced off its armour. Nearer and nearer the tank came, crushing scrub and rocks beneath its tracks. At last it was at the path. Onward it came, its great gun swinging down, pointing along the path. There was a BOOOOOM! and explosions as the shell from the tank detonated a series of mines on the path.

Marines ran from cover and took up positions behind the tank, crouching low, rifles at the ready. The tank lumbered on, defying the bullets of the Japanese snipers higher up the mountain. Their fire seemed less now. I assumed that our platoon had made an impact on their defences from inside the mountain. I wondered what had happened to Sergeant Sykes and the rest of our platoon.

As the tank reached us, the sergeant in charge ducked out from behind it and ran across to me and Paddy.

'OK, marine, what's the story?' he demanded.

'Pfc Smith from Fox Company, sir,' I responded. 'Our platoon has been inside the mountain, taking out Japanese defensive positions.'

The sergeant looked at us.

'Are you all that's left?'

'Hope not, sir,' I answered.

The sergeant nodded.

'OK,' he said. He turned to Paddy, 'Stay here until the corpsmen arrive. Smith, you're with us.'

For the rest of that day we were kept pinned down by Japanese fire. They rolled grenades at us down the mountain. They fired round after round at us. They let fly at us with mortar shells. But I could sense a new confidence among our troops. According to reports that were coming in, the other divisions had taken the airfield and were swarming north across the island, heading towards Airfield Number Two. As they went, they were mopping up, destroying the bunkers and pillboxes, digging out the enemy. Behind us, more marines were joining us, making their way up towards the mountain and airfields.

The Japanese weren't going to give up easily though. I turned and saw three marines making their way up the path caught in an explosion. When the smoke cleared, two of them were obviously dead, sprawled lifeless on the ground. The third was badly hurt and he was trying to drag himself away from the crater the explosion had made. He slumped down as a round hit him in his already shattered leg.

I looked around to see if anyone else was near enough to go to his aid, but we were the nearest unit.

'Sergeant!' I yelled. And I pointed to the wounded marine, struggling to get to cover, but pinned down by Japanese fire. 'Give me some covering fire. I'm gonna try and help that guy.'

The sergeant nodded.

'OK, guys!' he called. 'Start firing!'

While the rest of the unit opened up with their rifles, I ran and rolled as fast as I could back down the mountain until I reached the wounded marine.

'OK, buddy, let's get you under cover!' I said.

The marine looked at me and through the streaks of blood and dirt that spattered his face I was astonished to find myself looking at Henry Pelt.

'Krupp!' he gasped.

That nearly did it for me. Even in the heat of battle he had no respect for me. In my anger I was tempted to leave him right there. But I knew that I had to do the right thing – if only to prove finally to Henry that's what I was here for.

Getting into a crouch position, I grabbed him under the arms and began to haul him towards the cover of a large boulder. He whimpered, his shattered legs leaving a trail of blood. Once behind the boulder, I propped him up. Then I tore a strip off his uniform and tied makeshift tourniquets around his legs, just below the knees.

'There!' I grunted when I'd finished. 'You'll be OK if you don't move. Stay here until corpsmen get to you. They'll patch you up.'

I was turning to make the run back to my position, when I felt his hand grab me.

'John,' he said. 'I'm sorry.'

I turned, surprised because he had actually used my Christian name.

'Sorry for what?' I asked suspiciously.

'For calling you Krupp,' he said awkwardly. 'It was force of habit.' He gave a groan as the pain in his legs kicked in, but he gritted his teeth. 'And I'm sorry for the way I treated you when we were growing up. I never really believed you were a spy. I guess I was just jealous of you being so smart.' He forced a smile. 'In case I don't make it, I wanted to say thanks for helping me. You saved my life. I'll never doubt you again.'

'You'll make it,' I said gruffly.

Then I softened. All that anger I had felt for him over the years seemed to vanish as I looked at him, lying there so helpless and so apologetic.

'You always were a tough one, Henry,' I said. 'You'll make this.'

He nodded, and then held out his hand.

'Shake?' he asked.

'Sure,' I said. I took his hand and shook it firmly. 'Gotta go now.'

He released my hand with a nod. 'Go get 'em, John. See you back in Kalamazoo.'

I caught the sergeant's eye to let him

know I was coming back. He gave the order and they began the covering fire again. I gave one last grin to Henry and then began my scramble back up the rocks and scrub. As I did so, the Japanese opened up again.

This battle was still a long way from over.

Day began to turn into night, and still we hadn't advanced. The only good thing was the sight of Sergeant Sykes and some of our platoon stumbling out of the caves of Suribachi covered in dust and dirt. They dodged the Japanese fire to join us. After reporting to the commander of the company, Sykes came over to me.

'You got out, then,' he said.

I nodded. 'I was worried we'd lost you, sarge.'

'We got caught in a rock fall inside one of the caves. Lost some of the men. The rest of us managed to dig our way out.' He gave a grim smile. 'We managed to take out some of the enemy, though. How did you and Riley get on?'

I told him what had happened, and about Paddy being injured.

Sykes nodded. 'You've done a good job, Smith. I know how Saipan affected you.'

I looked away awkwardly, not knowing what to say.

'But you've faced the enemy again and you're alive,' he continued. 'That's what counts.'

As darkness fell, we kept to our dug-out positions, guns trained on the volcano, watching and waiting. How long could this go on for? How long could the Japanese hold out before their nerve cracked? I hadn't slept properly for four days. Tiredness was once again taking the place of fear. The order had been passed along the line to try and grab some sleep. It was going to be a big day tomorrow. So I took the chance to put my head down and close my eyes.

I hardly seemed to have had them shut for more than a few minutes, when the sounds of yells and shooting jerked me awake. The yelling was at close range, and it was in Japanese! We were being attacked!

Chapter 19
Raising the Flag

I snatched up my rifle, my head still fogged with sleep. We were in the middle of a Banzai attack! The Japanese must have come out of the caves under cover of darkness. Armed with bayonets, swords and hand-guns, they were hurling themselves at our positions, shrieking and yelling as they came. It was the same attitude as the kamikaze pilots. They were here to die and to take as many of us with them as they could.

The marines who'd been on watch had raised the alarm and were already opening fire. The rest of us joined in, firing as fast as we could as they came towards us.

The marine next to me fell down dead, taking a bullet through the head. I blasted away with my rifle.

Soon they were on us. At close range my

rifle was useless, except as a club. One Japanese hurled himself at me, the bayonet in his outstretched hand aimed at my face. I hit him hard with my rifle and he fell to the ground.

Then another threw himself at me, one of his arms grabbing me round my neck. His other hand held a bayonet and he was pulling it back to stab it into me. Sheer instinct and adrenalin took over. I dropped my rifle and grabbed the hand that held the bayonet. Desperately, I attacked him with the rest of my body: kicking him with my boots, using my knees, my one free elbow, even my head. It was like the worst kind of street fight, only here I knew the loser would die.

As I struggled, a kind of blind fury overtook me. I'd come all this way and I wasn't going to die at the hands of a Japanese soldier armed with just a bayonet.

Suddenly he went limp. I looked up and Sykes was standing there, bayonet in hand.

'Thank you,' I gasped and stood for a second, panting hard, my heart pounding inside my chest as if it was going to burst. I turned sharply, the Japanese bayonet now in my fist, crouching, waiting to be attacked again. But the attack was over.

None of us slept for the rest of that night. We were all on edge, expecting for another attack. But none came.

When dawn rose, we took stock of the situation. We had lost about twenty men. But lying across the base of Mount Suribachi, and sprawled at different points around our defences, were about two hundred dead Japanese. They'd paid dearly for their last-ditch desperate attack.

In the early morning light we continued our upward assault on the mountain, moving slowly, rock to rock, boulder to boulder, but this time we met little defensive fire. There was just the occasional sniper burst from the Japanese. It was as if the night-time banzai attack had been their last major throw of the dice – and they'd lost.

For the next four hours we advanced, knocking out pillboxes we came across. Higher and higher we climbed. I turned at one point and looked down from the mountain across the island. All over Iwo Jima there were marines, like ants on an ant-hill. Out at sea more and more landing-craft were coming in, with more reserves. The island was pitted with bomb-craters, ripped and torn apart. Tanks, bulldozers and other heavy machinery were crawling around. The invasion of Iwo Jima was gathering pace.

Then I turned to look back up the mountain and I felt a lump in my throat and tears came into my eyes. There, right up at the top of the mountain, the Stars and Stripes was being raised up on a pole.

'We did it!' muttered a voice next to me. 'We beat them!'

I turned. It was Sergeant Sykes. And I could see that in his eyes there were tears, too. Tears of pride at the sight of the flag fluttering there, on this island that had been considered an indestructible fortress.

I nodded, unable to speak. But my tears were not just for the sight of the flag being raised: they were for the men who'd died to make sure it was flown there – Redmond, Di Maggio, Compton, Vidor, and all those thousands of other marines I'd never

129

known. And for guys like Jimmy Wilson, who hadn't died, but had been traumatized by this nightmare.

And also, my tears were for me. I'd come through the danger and I'd faced my own fear. I'd survived and proved myself to be a worthy US marine.

Author's Note

Although this book is based on real events, additional action has been introduced for dramatic purposes, and also to show actualities of the Pacific campaign that were not apparent in the assault on Iwo Jima. This is particularly the case with the kamikaze attack. The fleet that attacked Iwo Jima was not subjected to kamikaze attacks. However, Japanese pilots did fly suicide missions against the American forces elsewhere and at other times in the Pacific campaign.

More than 2,000 kamikaze missions were flown against the US fleet at Okinawa. During April 1945 a further 1,400 suicide missions were flown in defence of Japanese home islands. These resulted in Allied losses of 26 ships sunk and 160 damaged.

The Battle for Iwo Jima and After

The battle for Iwo Jima was one of the bloodiest battles in the history of the US marines. Although the American flag was raised over Mount Suribachi on 23 February 1945, it was not until 16 March, after a further three weeks of battle, that Iwo Jima was declared secure. By the end of the conflict the casualty figures showed that out of a force of nearly 60,000 men, 5,391 US marines had been killed, with a further 17,400 wounded. About 2,500 of these casualties were on the first day of the landings. Of the Japanese defence force of 23,000, only 216 were taken alive.

The Significance of the Victory at Iwo Jima

● Heavy B-29 bomber losses over Japan emphasized the need for fighter escorts.

Since the 2,800-mile round-trip from US air-bases in the Marianas was beyond the range of fighters, a closer staging-point had to be captured.

Iwo Jima, with its completed air-bases and its close proximity to Tokyo (660 nautical miles or three hours' flying time) made an excellent base for Allied bombers.

● Once captured, Iwo Jima was a necessary and vital link in the air defences of the Marianas.

● Since Iwo Jima had traditionally been considered Japanese territory, and governed from Tokyo, its conquest was a severe psychological blow to the Japanese, as well as a vital strategic outpost denied to them.

Timetable of the Assault on Iwo Jima

1944

November - US navy bombards Iwo Jima for the first time.

December - US air force begins its 72-day bombardment of Iwo Jima. This was the longest and heaviest of the Pacific war. US navy/marine invasion force sets out for Iwo Jima.

1945

16 February - US navy begins a three-day concentrated bombing of Iwo Jima.

17 February - US frogmen suffer 170 casualties while investigating Iwo Jima's beach defences.

19 February - The 4th and 5th Marine Divisions land on Iwo Jima and gain a foothold.

23 February - Marines raise the US flag on summit of Mount Suribachi.

25 February - 3rd Marine Division is committed to the battle.

4 March - First B-29 bomber lands on Iwo Jima.

16 March - Iwo Jima is declared secure after 26 days of combat.

26 March - 300 Japanese, the last of the island's defenders, launch an early morning banzai charge against US marines, and are defeated.

7 April - B-29 bombers fly to Japan from Iwo Jima on a raid, escorted by P51 fighters.

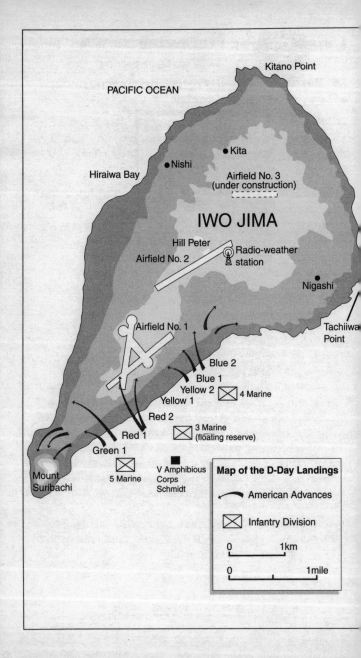

Kitano Point

PACIFIC OCEAN

● Kita

● Nishi

Hiraiwa Bay

Airfield No. 3
(under construction)

IWO JIMA

Hill Peter

Airfield No. 2

Radio-weather
station

● Nigashi

Tachiiwa
Point

Airfield No. 1

Blue 2

Blue 1

Yellow 2

Yellow 1

⊠ 4 Marine

Red 2

Red 1

⊠ 3 Marine
(floating reserve)

Green 1

⊠
5 Marine

Mount
Suribachi

■ V Amphibious
Corps
Schmidt

Map of the D-Day Landings

⌒ American Advances

⊠ Infantry Division

0   1km

0   1mile

Following in the
footsteps of
fighting heroes

June 1944 — D-day. Heavy fortifications on the
Normandy coast threaten the success of the Allied
operation. However, the British army has developed
secret armoured vehicles to pave a way through
the mines and trenches. A stroke of military
genius — or a death trap? One young driver
is about to discover the truth.

Part war story, part fact book, *Beach Assault*
reveals what it was really like to land and fight
in Normandy.

Collect the set

Following in the footsteps of fighting heroes

August 1943 — V2 rockets are a deadly threat to the Allied war effort. A fleet of 600 bombers sets out to destroy them and one young flight engineer prepares to risk his life in the most important mission he has ever flown.

Part war story, part fact book, *Night Bomber* reveals what it was really like to fly a Lancaster.

Collect the set